For the PDGSC—always fun, always delicious, always colorful!

BEACH LANE BOOKS • An imprint of Simon & Schuster Children's Publishing Division • 1230 Avenue of the Americas, New York, New York 10020 • Copyright © 2014 by Keith Baker • All rights reserved, including the right of reproduction in whole or in part in any form. • BEACH LANE BOOKS is a trademark of Simon & Schuster, Inc. • For information about special discounts for bulk purchases, please contact Simon & Schuster Special Sales at 1-866-506-1949 or business@simonandschuster.com. • The Simon & Schuster Speakers Bureau can bring authors to your live event. For more information or to book an event, contact the Simon & Schuster Speakers Bureau at 1-866-248-3049 or visit our website at www.simonspeakers.com. • Book design by Sonia Chaghatzbanian • The text for this book is set in Frankfurter Medium. • The illustrations for this book are rendered digitally. • Manufactured in China • 0514 SCP • First Edition • Library of Congress Cataloging-in-Publication Data • Baker, Keith, 1953– • Little green peas / Keith Baker.—First edition. • p. cm. • Summary: Little green peas make their way into collections of objects of many different colors, from blue boats, seas, and flags to orange balloons, umbrellas, and fizzy drinks. • ISBN 978-1-4424-7660-8 (hardcover) • ISBN 978-1-4424-7661-5 (eBook) • [1. Stories in rhyme. 2. Peas—Fiction. 3. Color—Fiction.] I. Title. • PZ8.3.B175Lj 2013 • [E]—dc23 • 2013019358 • 10 9 8 7 6 5 4 3 2 1

Keith Baker

LITTLE GREEN peas

a BIG book of COLORS

Beach Lane Books New York London Toronto Sydney New Delhi

Blue boats,   blue seas,

blue flags, and . . .

little green peas.

Red fences, red trees,

red kites, and . . .

little green peas.

Yellow buses—
                and bumblebees!

Yellow sun and . . .

little green peas.

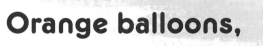

Orange balloons,

orange umbrellas,

orange bubbly drinks, and . . .

little green fellas.

Green vines, green leaves,

green sprouts, and . . .

baby green peas!

Purple mountains, purple skis,

purple mittens, and . . .

little green peas.

Silver coins, silver keys,

silver plates, and . . .

little green peas.

White stars, black skies—look!

What's that?

little green guys!